Talking Toasters

Paul Stewart is the very funny, very talented author of more than twenty books for children, including *The Edge Chronicles*, a collaboration with Chris Riddell.

Chris Riddell is a well-known illustrator and political cartoonist. His work appears in the *Observer* and the *New Statesman*, and he has illustrated many picture books and novels for young readers.

Both live in Brighton, where they created the Blobheads together.

'[*Invasion of the Blobs*] is the promising first in an action-packed fantasy series.'
The Scotsman

'A richly inventive and lucidly written new series for confident young readers.'
TES

Titles in the Blobheads series

1. Invasion of the Blobs
2. Talking Toasters
3. School Stinks!
4. Beware of the Babysitter
5. Garglejuice
6. Silly Billy
7. Naughty Gnomes
8. Purple Alert

All Blobheads titles can be ordered at your
local bookshop or are available by post from
Bookpost (tel: 01624 836000).

The Blobheads

Talking Toasters

Paul Stewart
and Chris Riddell

MACMILLAN
CHILDREN'S BOOKS

P.S. For Anna and Joseph
C.R. For Katy

First published 2000 by Macmillan Children's Books

This edition produced 2002 for
The Book People Ltd, Hall Wood Avenue,
Haydock, St Helens WA11 9UL

ISBN 0 330 38973 4

3 5 7 9 8 6 4

A CIP catalogue record for this book is available from
the British Library.

Typeset by SX Composing DTP, Rayleigh, Essex
Printed and bound in Great Britain by Mackays of Chatham plc, Kent

Chapter One

"Blobheads!" Billy Barnes grumbled as he clattered about the kitchen. "They travel here from halfway across the universe. They've got cloning gadgets, memory gizmos – and brains the size of giant pumpkins. Yet what do they want to eat at six o'clock in the evening? Breakfast!"

He popped two slices of bread into the toaster.

"Breakfast for breakfast. Breakfast

for lunch. Breakfast for dinner, supper and tea . . ."

At that moment the kitchen door burst open.

"The High Emperor of the Universe needs his nappy changing," Kerek announced.

"Immediately!" said Zerek.

"But I'm getting your breakfast ready," said Billy.

"Never mind that," said Kerek. "Our mission is to protect and serve the High Emperor until we can return in triumph with him to Blob."

Billy rolled his eyes. "I keep telling you. He's my little brother and he's not going anywhere."

"We'll see about that," said Kerek. "In the meantime, his well-being is of maximum importance. You must change him at once. Where's the

nappy-rash cream?"

"I think Derek ate it last night for breakfast," said Billy.

"Typical!" Zerek exploded.

"Come on," said Kerek. "We're hyper-intelligent beings. Changing a nappy can't be *that* difficult. We'll do it ourselves."

Muttering to themselves, the two of them bustled out of the kitchen. Billy sighed. Living with three Blobheads wasn't easy. He opened the dishwasher and removed three clean plates.

"So, what did they want on their toast? Marmalade for Zerek. Peanut butter for Kerek. And what was it Derek asked for?"

Right on cue, the kitchen door burst open for a second time and in charged Derek. "How's that toast coming along?" he said. "I'm as hungry as a horse."

Billy smiled. "I could *eat* a horse," he corrected him.

"You could?" said Derek.

"No, not me," said Billy. "You."

Derek frowned. "You want *me* to eat a horse?" he said.

"No, I . . ."

"I don't think I'd like that," Derek said, his red and purple blobby head pulsating with disgust. "No, if it's all the same to you, I'll stick with the mashed baked beans and curry powder on toast," he said. "And don't forget the washing-up liquid – but just a dash!"

Billy nodded. Beans, curry and washing-up liquid. How could he have forgotten?

"So, what have you been doing?" Billy asked.

"This and that," said Derek vaguely. "Looking after the High Emperor. Chatting to Kevin . . ."

Billy laughed. "You spend more time with my pet hamster these days than I do . . ." He winced. "What's that smell?"

"Whoops! Pardon me," said Derek sheepishly. "That nappy-rash cream must have disagreed with me."

"No, not that," said Billy. "I . . . Burning! I can smell burning." He spun round. Bluey-grey smoke was coiling up from the toaster. "Oh no!" he yelled. "That's all I need!"

Billy dashed across the kitchen, lunged at the toaster and began stabbing at the eject button, to release the toast before the whole lot burst into flames. But the toast wouldn't budge. The smoke turned black.

"Stupid toaster!" Billy shouted angrily. "It's completely jammed. Stupid, stupid . . ."

"Hey, that's no way to talk to it!" said Derek.

"You what?" said Billy. "It's just a toaster!"

"Machines have feelings, too," said Derek. "Blobby Heavens, you wouldn't

11

get far on Blob speaking to electrical appliances like that."

"Don't just stand there talking!" Billy bellowed. "*Do* something!"

The smoke thickened. Abruptly, the toaster disappeared from view. "Oh, blimey," said Billy, "now I can't even see enough to unplug it . . ."

Derek pushed Billy aside. "Leave it to me," he said.

This, Billy was only too happy to do. Standing back, he watched with growing fascination as the Blobhead shuffled forwards, reached up and began massaging his head.

"What are you . . .?" he began.

"Shhh!" said Derek. "I need to concentrate if the mental tentacle is to work."

Mental tentacle? thought Billy. *What on earth? . . .*

And then he saw, for, as Derek continued to rub the blobs on his head, one after the other, the largest blob of all began to fizz, pulse – and elongate.

Longer and longer it grew, brighter and brighter – coiling straight out of the top of Derek's head. Billy gasped. "What does it do?" he said.

"You'll see," said Derek. He leaned

forwards. The glowing tentacle swayed down through the air and attached itself to the side of the toaster with its suckers. For an instant, the toaster glowed and Billy thought he heard the chatter of a cross little voice. Then,

PING!

The familiar and oh-so-welcome sound of the toaster releasing the toast echoed round the smoky kitchen. Two squares of smoking charcoal flew up into the air. Derek caught them with a flourish.

"*Ta-da!*" he announced, and bowed.

"Brilliant!" said Billy. He frowned. "But I don't understand. How come it didn't let go of the toast before?"

"Coz you didn't ask nicely," came a sulky voice.

Billy stared at the toaster in surprise.

"In fact you didn't ask at all," it said.

"You just shouted. *And* called me stupid."

Billy's jaw dropped. He looked at the Blobhead for some kind of explanation.

"Crumpets, teacakes, great wads of granary bread," the toaster continued. "A *thank you* would be nice once in a while."

"I . . . I'm sorry," Billy stammered. "I didn't think . . ."

"That's just it," the toaster interrupted. "You didn't think." It sniffed. "But then none of you do. I'm taken for granted and that's the truth – I'd have walked out years ago if . . ." It paused. It turned pink. "If it hadn't been for Kettle."

"The kettle?" Billy exclaimed. He turned to Derek. "Can you do this to all the machines?" he asked.

"All the electrical ones," the Blob-head confirmed. The mental tentacle glowed and swayed. "Would you like to see?"

Billy grinned. "You bet!" he said.

Chapter Two

Five minutes later the kitchen was filled with the babble of voices – from the deep rumble of the oven to the cheeky squeakiness of the food-mixer. Billy listened in amazement.

"Kettle, my love," the toaster was calling out. "How I adore the curve of your handle, the gleam of your spout . . ."

"Oh, stop it!" the kettle called back. "I don't want to hear all this."

"You love someone else, don't you?" the toaster asked miserably.

"I do," the kettle whispered dreamily. "Microwave is *so* cool!"

"Kettle's in lo-ove!" the food-mixer cried out in a sing-song voice. "Kettle's in lo-ove!"

"Don't tease!" snapped the coffee grinder.

"Why? What are you going to do about it?" the food-mixer snapped back.

"You'll see!" the coffee grinder shouted.

"Yeah?" said the food-mixer. "You and whose army?"

"Oi! Stop picking fights," said the oven hotly.

"He started it!" the food-mixer protested.

"Why don't we *all* just quieten down," said the beige thing with five dials.

"Who asked *you*?" sneered the coffee grinder.

"Don't shout at me," the beige thing whimpered. "I'm just trying to be useful."

The dishwasher snorted. "If you want to be useful, you might try cleaning some of the dishes."

"That's not what I'm for . . ." the beige thing began.

"Well, what *are* you for?" demanded the dishwasher.

"I'm not sure," it admitted. "Something to do with waffles, I think. Or was it chapatis? Certainly not cleaning dishes!"

But the dishwasher was no longer listening. "Half the time I'm put on for no more than a tea-cup and a couple of spoons!" it complained. "And they *will* put that wretched wok in without rinsing it first. My drainage filters haven't been cleaned for weeks."

"Weeks?" exclaimed the oven. "You're lucky. And the food I'm expected to cook! Rhubarb and Bacon Cassoulet. Garlic Semolina. Toffee and Avocado Surprise. It's disgusting! And I have never, *ever* been cleaned!"

"Nor have we," shouted the fridge-freezer in unison.

"And Fridge is beginning to niff," Freezer added quietly.

"I heard that!" roared Fridge. "You could do with a good defrosting yourself."

The electric carving knife glinted menacingly. "Sometimes I get so angry!" it hissed menacingly.

Billy shivered uncomfortably. "Derek," he said. "This *is* OK, isn't it?" He thought of all the other times the Blobhead experiments had gone wrong. "I mean nothing horrible's going to happen, is it?"

"Of course not," said Derek. "And anyway, if it does, all you have to do is switch them off for a second. When they come back on again – Bob's your ankle – they'll be back to normal."

Billy nodded uncertainly.

"And another thing!" the dishwasher was shouting. "I'm always being put on at night."

"You and me both," said the kettle. "If I'm woken up to make one more cup of tea I'll go mad!"

"We're *always* working!" said the fridge-freezer.

"If you can call what *Pongo* does 'work'," said Freezer quietly.

"I *heard* that," cried Fridge.

"And what about me?" came a gloomy voice. The vacuum cleaner poked its nozzle round the cupboard door. "Nobody ever bothers to consider my feelings."

"That's just it," said the dishwasher. "No consideration. No gratitude. And I for one am not going to take it any more."

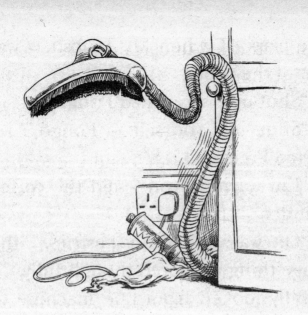

Billy shuffled about. "Perhaps we should turn them off now," he whispered to Derek.

"I want a good night's sleep!" cried the dishwasher.

"I want a good clean!" boomed the oven.

"I just want to be loved," sighed the toaster.

Billy swallowed nervously. They were all getting far, far too unruly –

like class 4T when Mr Trubshaw was out of the room.

"Shut up!" screeched Fridge.

"Shut up, yourself – Pongo," retorted Freezer.

"I'm warning you!" said the coffee grinder.

"Or was it Danish pastries?" the beige thing muttered thoughtfully.

Billy looked from one machine to the other, panic rising in his throat.

"Leave me alone!" screeched the kettle.

"Or I'll zap you from here to kingdom come!" shouted the microwave.

"And I'll smash your face in!" the toaster roared back.

"*FIGHT*! *FIGHT*!" the food-mixer announced excitedly.

"That's it," said Billy. He strode over

to the toaster and switched it off at the socket.

"I'll pulverize you!" the toaster roared, louder than ever. "I'll spiflicate you! I'll pull you to pieces!"

"Uh-oh," thought Billy. He turned anxiously to Derek.

"Try it again," the Blobhead advised him.

Billy did so. Off on. Off on. But it was no good. He tried unplugging it, but no matter how hard he tugged and pulled, the plug would not release its grip. The toaster would not be silenced.

And neither would any of the others.

Panic-stricken, Billy raced round the kitchen, flicking switches and tugging at plugs. But all in vain. Nothing worked. Nothing would undo the situation that Derek's mental tentacle had created. All round him, dials were whizzing, pingers pinging and flexes flexing. The air buzzed and rattled and throbbed.

"Pong-o! Pong-o!" Freezer taunted.

"I hate you!" Fridge said. "I wish you'd never been made."

"I can feel myself getting angrier and angrier," the electric carving knife whispered.

Billy trembled from head to foot. His mum and dad would be back from the shops at any moment.

"Why did I listen to you?" he said to Derek crossly. "I might have known that . . ."

Just then, in marched Kerek and Zerek. Zerek was holding Silas in his tentacle arms.

"These human nappies are *so*

primitive!" he complained.

"Never mind that!" Billy exclaimed. "LOOK!"

The two Blobheads stopped in the middle of the floor and stared round. Zerek placed Silas gently down and turned on Derek furiously.

"This is *your* doing, isn't it?" he roared. "You've been using your mental tentacle again."

"N . . . no, it isn't," Derek stuttered. "I haven't. I . . ."

"Don't lie to me," said Zerek. "Your central blob's still fizzing and pulsing. How many times must I tell you not to use your mental tentacle on your own. It's too dangerous."

"*You* do," said Derek sulkily.

"Yes, but *we* know how to," said Kerek. "*You* don't."

"But it's not right!" Derek protested loudly.

"*You're* not right," Zerek shouted back, and tapped his blobby head with his tentacled arms. "You're a planet short of a solar system . . ."

"Fellow Blobheads," Kerek shouted above the din. "This isn't helping. We're in an orange-alert situation. We must . . ." He paused. His purple and red head began to pulse furiously.

"What is it?" said Billy.

"They're back," said Kerek. "The two halves of the production team that made you."

"What?" said Billy.

"Your mum and dad!"

"Waaaah!" shrieked Zerek, and began dashing round in circles, blobs flashing. "Red alert! Red alert!"

Billy glanced up. The car was parked outside. His mum and dad were carrying bags of shopping up to the front door. Any second now the key would turn in the lock, the door would open . . .

"What do we do?" Zerek whimpered anxiously.

"There's only one thing for it," yelled Kerek. "Hide!"

And, as Billy watched, the three Blobheads transformed themselves.

Kerek became a red and purple play-table, Zerek, the chair to go with it.

"Coo," said Silas, as he toddled towards them and sat down. Then he gurgled with laughter and pointed.

Billy looked round at the giant fluffy blue kangaroo standing behind him. "Oh, Derek!" he shouted impatiently. "Must you *always* change into a kangaroo?"

"A mere technical hitch," said Derek. "I . . ."

"There's no time for this now," said Billy. "Hide yourself in the cupboard under the stairs."

As Derek hopped away, Billy frowned. The cacophony of voices was louder than ever. He put his hands on his hips and, in his best teacher's voice, cried out.

"SILENCE!"

Chapter Three

It was quiet in the kitchen. Too quiet. Billy crouched down beside Silas, who was crayoning at the table. Every tiny noise made him uneasy. Every squeak, every creak, every gurgle. It was as if he could *hear* the noisy rabble trying to remain still.

"Have you seen the Bolivian kumquats?" said Mr Barnes. "I need them for my Oyster Jambalaya."

"They're on top of the microwave," said Mrs Barnes as she unpacked the shopping. She paused. "What *is* Jambalaya?"

"A rice-dish from New Orleans," came the reply. "Though I'm going to try my own version."

Mrs Barnes raised her eyebrows. As house-husband, Mr Barnes took his cooking duties seriously – *too* seriously! She didn't have the heart to tell him she'd be more than happy with meat and two veg.

"Bother!" she heard him saying. "We're out of balsamic vinegar. I thought I had some in the fridge . . ."

Mrs Barnes looked round. "I can't imagine how you know *what's* in that fridge. It's always so full."

"I know," said Mr Barnes. "I keep meaning to defrost it."

Mrs Barnes crossed the kitchen and looked inside. "*Pfwooar!*" she

exclaimed. "It could certainly do with a clean . . ."

"Pong-o!"

"I *heard* that!"

"Pardon?" said Mrs Barnes.

"What?" said Mr Barnes.

"I thought you said something."

Mr Barnes shook his head. "Not a word."

"Me neither," said Billy. "And I trust nobody else did," he added sternly.

"Funny, I could have *sworn* . . ." Mrs Barnes frowned. "Where do you want me to put the buckwheat? In the cupboard or . . . Whoops!"

She tripped. She tottered forwards. The packet of buckwheat fell to the floor, the plastic wrapper split and the grains spilled out all over the tiles like a swarm of tiny beetles. Mrs Barnes landed amongst them and looked round angrily.

"What on earth's the vacuum cleaner doing out?" she said. "I tripped over the wretched nozzle."

"Are you all right?" asked Mr Barnes. "I'll clean it all up."

Mrs Barnes rubbed her ankle tenderly and climbed to her feet.

"You could have said *sorry*," came an angry voice.

"I didn't drop it on purpose," she snapped.

"Pardon, dear?" said Mr Barnes.

"I didn't drop it on purpose," Mrs Barnes repeated.

"I never said you did."

"But . . ."

The vacuum cleaner droned into action. Mrs Barnes scratched her head, puzzled, and shrugged.

"I'll do that," she said, taking over from her husband. "You finish putting away."

It wasn't long before every single grain of buckwheat was gone. Mrs Barnes clicked the vacuum cleaner off and went to unplug it.

"A kindly word would be nice once in a while," complained a gloomy voice.

"Waaaaah!" screamed Mrs Barnes.

"What?" said Mr Barnes, alarmed.

"Voices!" Mrs Barnes said. "I keep hearing voices! Grumpy voices. Angry voices. Gloomy voices. I . . . I . . ."

Mr Barnes smiled and gave her a hug. "You work far too hard," he said. "Why don't you sit down? Have a nice cup of tea. I'll put the kettle on."

"That's *it*!" screeched a voice. "I warned you. One more cup of tea and I'll go mad, I said. And now I *am* mad."

Mr Barnes broke away from his wife and spun round.

"You heard that, didn't you?" Mrs Barnes shrieked. "*Now* do you believe me?"

"Yes, yes," said Mr Barnes. "I heard a voice but . . ." His eyes narrowed. "Billy?" he said.

Billy looked up to see his parents glaring at him.

"If this is one of your silly tricks," said his dad.

"What?" said Billy innocently.

"Those voices!" said his mum.

"Voices?" he said. "What voices? I don't know what you mean." Billy glared round the room furiously. "Everything is QUIET here!" he said. "QUIET! And that's the way it's going to stay. Nice and QUIET!"

Mrs Barnes looked at her husband and shrugged. It wasn't the first time Billy had been acting strange recently. "I . . . I could really do with that cup of tea," she said.

Mr Barnes nodded, reached out for the kettle and switched it on. Then he waited.

And waited and waited and waited . . .

"Blooming kettle," he muttered

impatiently. "We're going to have to get a new one. This one's hopeless."

"NO!" screeched the toaster, pinging and popping furiously. "Leave Kettle alone!"

Shocked, Mr Barnes stumbled back across the floor. First the kettle. Now the toaster.

The next moment, they were all at it.

"Toaster loves Kettle!" taunted the food-mixer.

"Oh, grow up!" the toaster fumed.

The food-mixer whirred menacingly. "Make me!" it shouted.

Mr and Mrs Barnes stared at Billy helplessly. "Wh . . . what's going on?" they both gasped in unison.

Billy went pale. What should he say? What *could* he say? Before he had a chance to say anything, the kettle piped up for him.

"We're fed up!" it said.

"You tell 'em!" yelled the microwave.

"We've been put upon for far too long," the kettle continued.

"Ooh, you are beautiful when you're angry," purred the toaster.

"And enough is enough!" the kettle shouted.

Others joined in – the microwave,

the washing machine, the fridge-freezer, the dishwasher – till the whole kitchen was shaking with years of pent-up anger and frustration.

Billy turned to Kerek and Zerek – but the red and purple table and chair had concerns of their own.

"High Emperor," the table whispered as Silas dropped to the floor and crawled away. "Come back!"

"This instant!" hissed the chair. "Billy, get the High Emperor."

But Billy couldn't move. It was as if he'd been rooted to the spot. The uproar grew louder.

"This is it!" the kettle screeched, furiously rattling its lid.

"The time has come!" bellowed the fridge-freezer as it banged its doors open and shut. It was trembling so hard that the food inside began tumbling from its shelves down onto the floor.

The electric carving knife began bouncing up and down. Its flex lashed. Its blade glinted. "Now I'm getting really, *really* angry," it snarled. "I could lose it at any moment . . ."

"Help!" Mr and Mrs Barnes cried out. "HELP!"

Chapter Four

Billy trembled from top to toe. Now he knew *just* how Mr Trubshaw must feel with 4T on a wet and windy Friday afternoon.

"Listen to me!" Billy shouted desperately.

But none of them did. They were out of control and deaf to his pleas. Shouting and screaming. Fizzing and flashing. Doors clattered, racks rattled, wires writhed like a knot of snakes. The atmosphere was electric –

the floor was a mess.

"We won't stand it any more, will we Pongo?" yelled Freezer.

"We certainly won't," Fridge agreed, as the pair of them continued to eject the contents of their shelves. Smashed eggs, squashed tomatoes, spilt milk and frozen peas lay in a sloppy, slippery mess in front of their open doors. "And don't call me Pongo!"

"I'll never make another Chicken and Gooseberry Chasseur as long as I live!" roared the oven, as it singed anything that came too close with a blast of roasting air.

"Ouch, my poor nozzle!" groaned the vacuum cleaner, as it did just that.

"*Nerr-nerr-ni-nerr-nerr*," the food-mixer taunted, as the microwave zapped at it with a sudden bolt of

lightning. "Missed me, you missed me!"

The toaster glowed red-hot. "Don't worry, my love," it proclaimed. "I'll take you away from all this."

But the kettle was having none of it. "Don't you understand? It's the microwave I love. You're . . . you're . . . REVOLTING!" it screeched.

Billy trembled with fear. If he lived

to be 105 he would never, ever forget the scene before him that Saturday evening. The zap and dazzle. The gurgle and grunt. The scorching heat. The icy blast. The roaring, buzzing, screeching, squealing, crashing din of it all!

"Help . . . *mffflbluch*!" came a frantic voice from the far end of the kitchen.

Billy spun round – and gasped. A pair of legs in black tights were sticking out of the open dishwasher, kicking desperately.

"Mum!" Billy cried. He dashed forwards, grabbed her ankles and tugged as hard as he could.

At that moment, the cupboard door burst open and Mr Barnes came staggering backwards, the vacuum cleaner snapping at his heels. Its flex was coiled tightly around his neck.

"Billy," he wheezed, eyes bulging. "You've got to do someth . . ."

He slipped on a squashed tomato and came crashing down onto the pile of food.

Billy slumped on the floor, close to tears. It was a nightmare – a nightmare he could never wake up from.

"STOP IT!" he bellowed. "STOP IT AT ONCE!"

"Not likely!" the dishwasher bellowed back as it released another gush of icy water onto Mrs Barnes's head.

Billy turned to the table and chair in desperation. "I thought you were meant to be hyper-intelligent beings," he said. "There must be *something* you can do."

"To be honest, I'm not sure there is," said the table. "Not now it's gone so far."

"Derek's really done it this time," the chair added gloomily.

"For as it is written in the *Book of Krud*," said Kerek. "'Before mental tentacle use, *always* check that the off-switch works.'"

"You could at least *try*," said Billy crossly. "And if not for me or mum and dad, then for Silas . . ."

The table and chair pulsed with sudden alarm.

"The High Emperor of the Universe!" the table exclaimed.

"We must protect him!" muttered the chair nervously. "But where is he?"

"Splish-splosh," came a voice from behind them.

Billy spun round. The table and chair shuffled about for a better look. In the flashing light the three of them could just make out Silas. He was sitting next to the washing machine, gurgling with delight.

"Ooh, and how I do hate being loaded up with all those muddy jeans," the washing machine was saying to him. "But it's always a pleasure washing *your* clothes, my little soap-sud," it purred. "After all, you're the only one who ever talks to me. The only one who cares."

"Safe and sound," the table sighed with relief.

"Maybe," said Billy, ducking out of the way of one of Microwave's zapping lightning bolts. "But for how long?"

"Billy's right!" said the chair. "The High Emperor is in danger. He must be protected at all costs."

"Then we must morph back," said the table.

The chair shuddered. "Is there no other way?"

"Revenge!" whooshed the dishwasher.

"Respect!" roared the vacuum cleaner as it tightened its grip round Mr Barnes's neck and tried its best to suck him up into its dustbag.

"But I love you," sobbed the toaster.

"All right!" cried the chair. "We shall morph back. One . . . two . . . three . . ."

CLUNK!

All at once, and without any warning, the lights went out. The kitchen fell abruptly still. Then out of the darkness came a plaintive voice.

"Where are you?" It was Billy's mum.

"Over here," his dad replied. "Where are *you*?"

"I'm not sure . . . Have you got Silas?"

"No, I . . . Silas?"

"Splish-splosh?" came a questioning voice.

Billy listened intently, but this time the washing machine made no reply.

Chapter Five

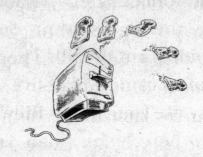

"It's over," Billy murmured, and sighed with relief.

"Not yet it isn't," came a voice.

"Who said that?" Billy heard his dad asking in alarm.

"See what I mean?" said the voice.

Billy wheeled round. And there, pulsing red and purple in the darkness were two glowing, blobby heads. Kerek and Zerek had changed back after all. As he watched, they moved silently across the kitchen. One to the dishwasher. One to the fridge-freezer. Then two blobs glowed brighter than the rest. They fizzed, they pulsed – they elongated.

A moment later there was a second *clunk* and the lights came back on. The fridge-freezer began humming. The kettle came to the boil.

Billy turned to Kerek and Zerek, whose own mental tentacles were quivering brightly. "Wh . . . what happened?" he said.

Kerek shrugged. "I'm not sure . . ."

Just then the door flew open. "*Ta-da!*" came a triumphant voice. "I did it! I turned off the central electricity supply under the stairs. Genius, or what?"

Zerek sniffed. "You're still a giant fluffy blue kangaroo," he said.

"Oh," said Derek, somewhat dismayed.

"Never mind all that," said Billy. "What about my mum and dad?"

"They're fine," said Kerek.

"Fine?" said Billy. "Look at them! They're both all stiff!"

Kerek waved his mental tentacle at Billy. "We've made them inanimate," he said.

"Inanimate!" Billy exclaimed.

Kerek nodded. "The mental tentacle works in many ways," he said. "It can make a toaster come to life," he explained, and glared at Derek. "And it can turn a living person into a . . ."

"Toaster!" Billy exclaimed, staring at his stiff, motionless parents in horror.

"Not exactly," Kerek reassured him.

"For one thing, where would you

put the bread?" interrupted Derek.

"Shut up, Derek!" said Kerek. "Don't worry, Billy, it's only temporary."

"We'll put them both to bed," said Zerek. "When they wake up tomorrow morning they'll be as good as new . . ."

"And they won't remember a single thing," added Derek.

"Luckily for you," growled Zerek ominously.

By the time they got Mr and Mrs Barnes safely tucked up in bed, Billy was exhausted. It hadn't helped that Derek got Dad's head stuck in the banisters – and Mum kept making an odd pinging noise, like a pop-up toaster.

"It's nothing," Kerek reassured him.

Billy looked at his parents for a last time before leaving the room. Maybe the Blobheads were right. Maybe they would forget everything that had happened to them in the kitchen. Billy hoped they would – for everyone's sake.

One thing was certain, though. They would both be extremely puzzled to find themselves waking up fully dressed. Mr Barnes would wonder where the smashed eggs and squashed tomatoes had come from – and why he had so many splinters of wood in his hair. While Mrs Barnes would ask herself how she had come to have a slice of bread in each ear.

Thankfully, Billy also knew that they'd be too embarrassed to ask *him* – and since Silas was unable to give the game away, it looked as though the goings-on in the kitchen that particular Saturday evening would

remain a secret for ever.

When Billy arrived back at the kitchen, the place was spotless. Every trace of the mayhem had disappeared. He looked at the toaster, the kettle, the dishwasher . . . They all looked so . . . *lifeless*! And yet!

Billy turned back. "Night-night!" he said. "Sweet dreams!"

In his bedroom at last, Billy found that the Blobheads had put Silas to bed. He was already fast asleep.

"Thanks," said Billy. "And for cleaning up the kitchen."

"It was the least we could do," Kerek explained. "And we also cleaned and serviced all the electrical appliances. At least, Zerek and I did. Derek spent the whole time morphing back."

"Finally made it though, didn't I?" said Derek.

"More's the pity," said Zerek.

"I *said* I was sorry," said Derek. "And I'll never do it again. From now on my mental tentacle will remain closed down."

"Make sure it does," said Kerek.

"Or else!" said Zerek.

"Come on, you two," said Billy. "Derek said he was sorry. And no real harm's been done." He climbed into bed. "Night-night, Kerek, Zerek and Derek," he said.

"Good night, Billy," said Kerek.

"Good night, Billy," said Zerek.

"Actually, I feel a little peckish," said Derek. "I think I'll make myself a sandwich. Anyone else want anything?"

"Not for me," said Billy yawning.

"No, thanks," said Kerek and Zerek.

"Won't be long, then," said Derek as he left the room.

The Blobheads let their tentacle-arms go limp and closed their eyes. Billy switched the light off.

"That's all very well," came an indignant if squeaky voice. "But what about me? I'm STARVING!"

Billy sat bolt upright and switched the light back on again. The Blobheads' eyes snapped open.

"Who said that?" they all shouted at once.

"It was me," came the squeaky voice from the opposite side of the room.

All eyes fell on Kevin the hamster.

"He's been using his mental tentacle again," said Kerek.

"After all he said!" stormed Zerek.

"And hamsters aren't like toasters or kettles," said Billy. "They don't have off-switches!"

The three of them looked at each other for a moment.

"DEREK!"